Emily's Numbers

Joss Langford

For Robyn & Seb.

First published in Great Britain by Arch Interface in 2018

ISBN 978-1-9999475-0-7

www.archinterface.co.uk/emily

A story of how the primes,
accidentally, came to be.

Emily loved to count.

Words were good for saying what you wanted for tea or writing a list for Father Christmas.

But counting was what Emily loved best.

Starting at one, she would list numbers of anything and everything. Bubbles, cars, fallen leaves, sea gulls, pebbles, anything.

1, 2, 3, 4, 5, 6, 7 …

… 207, 208, 209 …

Emily's counting numbers are positive integers. The word 'integer' originates from the Latin *integer*, meaning whole, and has been in use for nearly 500 years.

One day, when searching for every pair of shoes in the house, Emily began counting in twos.

2, 4, 6, 8, 10, 12, 14 …

She knew about odd and even numbers.

Emily discovered that, starting with two, she could create a list of just the even numbers and another of the odd numbers.

Her usual counting numbers split perfectly into two equal lists.

The word 'even' came to be used in the context of numbers in the 16th century. It is derived from the Old English *efen*, meaning level, equal or calm.

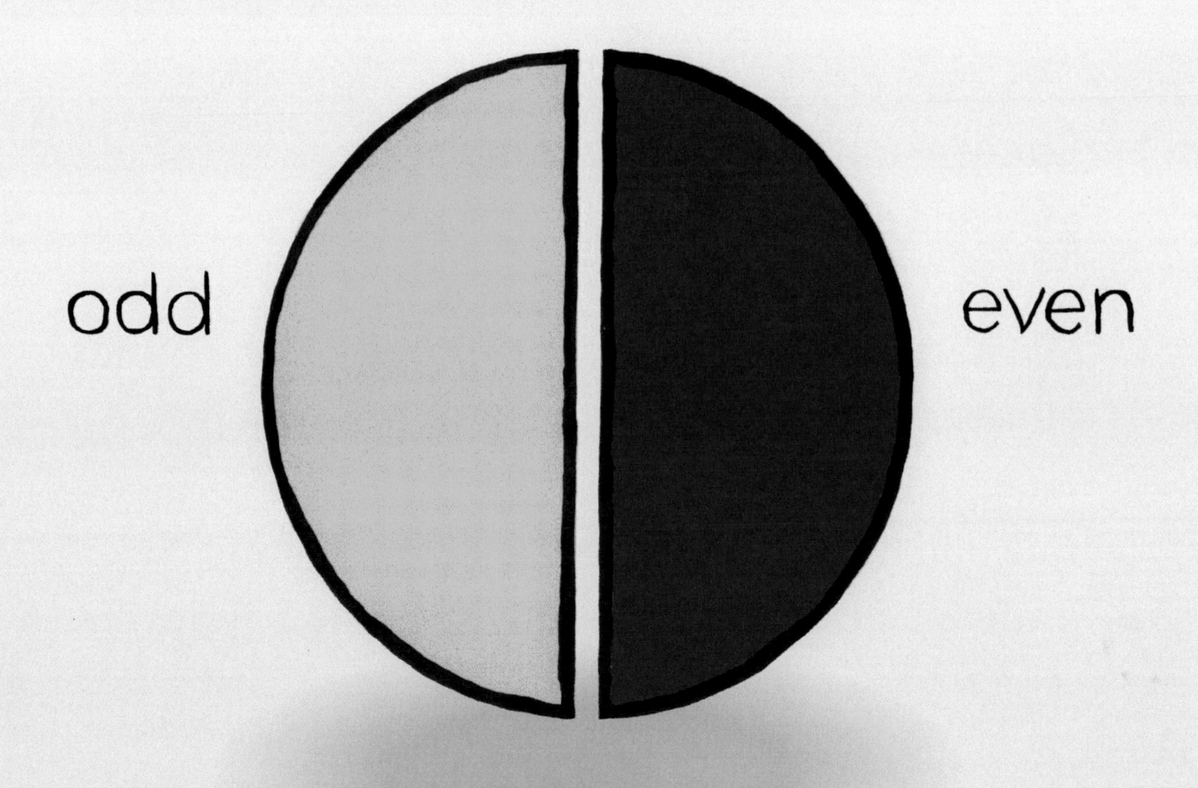

'Odd' stems from the Old Norse *oddi*, meaning third number, triangle or point and has been in use since the 13th century. Although there are an infinite number of integers, they are all represented above.

Emily wondered if three could also have a list of its own and began counting in threes.

She noticed that half of the threes were the same numbers she had just counted in the even list.

The odd numbers seemed more interesting. So Emily made the list with only these new numbers.

3, ~~6,~~ 9, ~~12,~~ 15, ~~18,~~
21, ~~24,~~ 27, ~~30,~~ 33 …

This list needed a name and Emily chose to call it threeven.

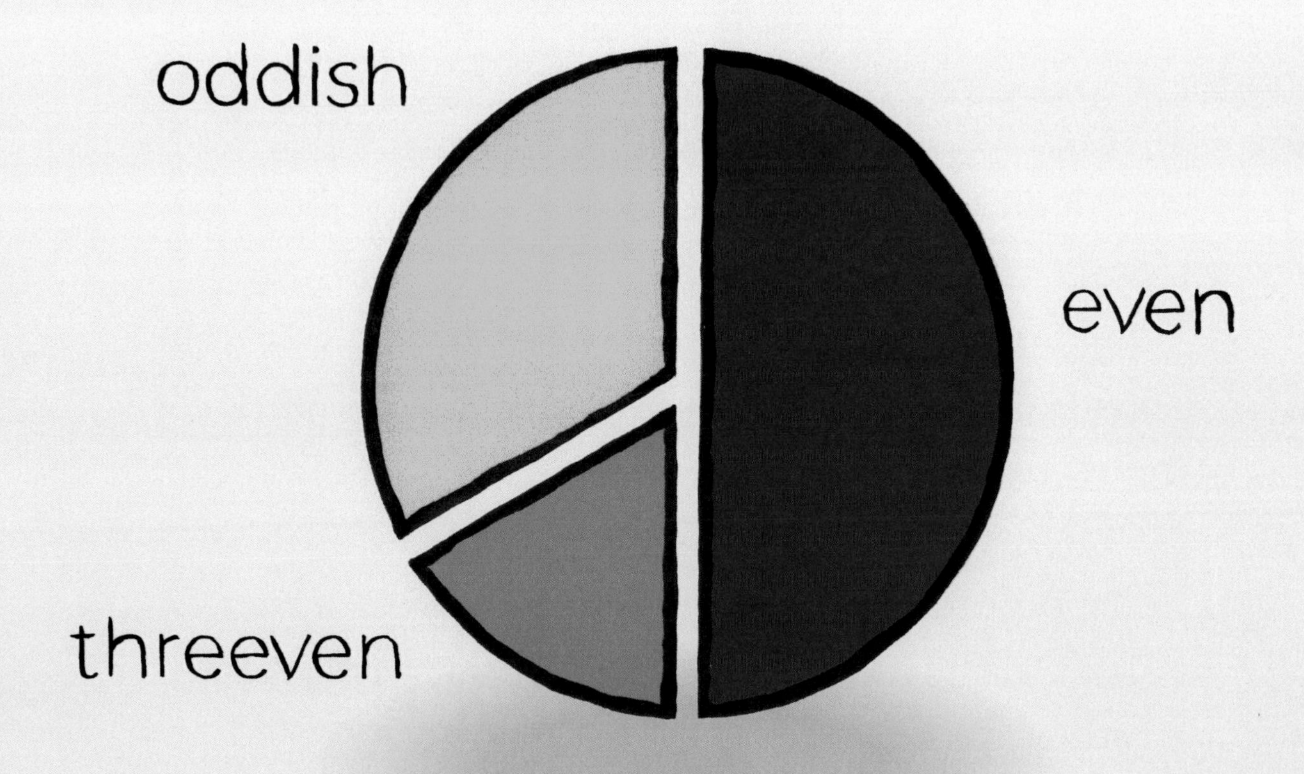

The remaining numbers, with the evens and threevens removed, were no longer the odd numbers. But they were similar - oddish.

This new representation still holds all the integers - each with a unique position in just one of the segments. The threeven numbers are a subset of the odd numbers.

Pleased with her success on the threeven list, Emily decided to try her luck with the next number.

Four proved difficult. When counting in fours, all the numbers were even and Emily could not make a new list.

Disappointed, Emily tried five, with better results. A fifth of the most recent oddish numbers were products of five and a new list was born!

5, 25, 35, 55, 65, 85 …

'Product' describes the result of multiplication and is derived from the Latin *productum*, meaning something produced. First seen in mathematics in the 15th century before coming into more general use.

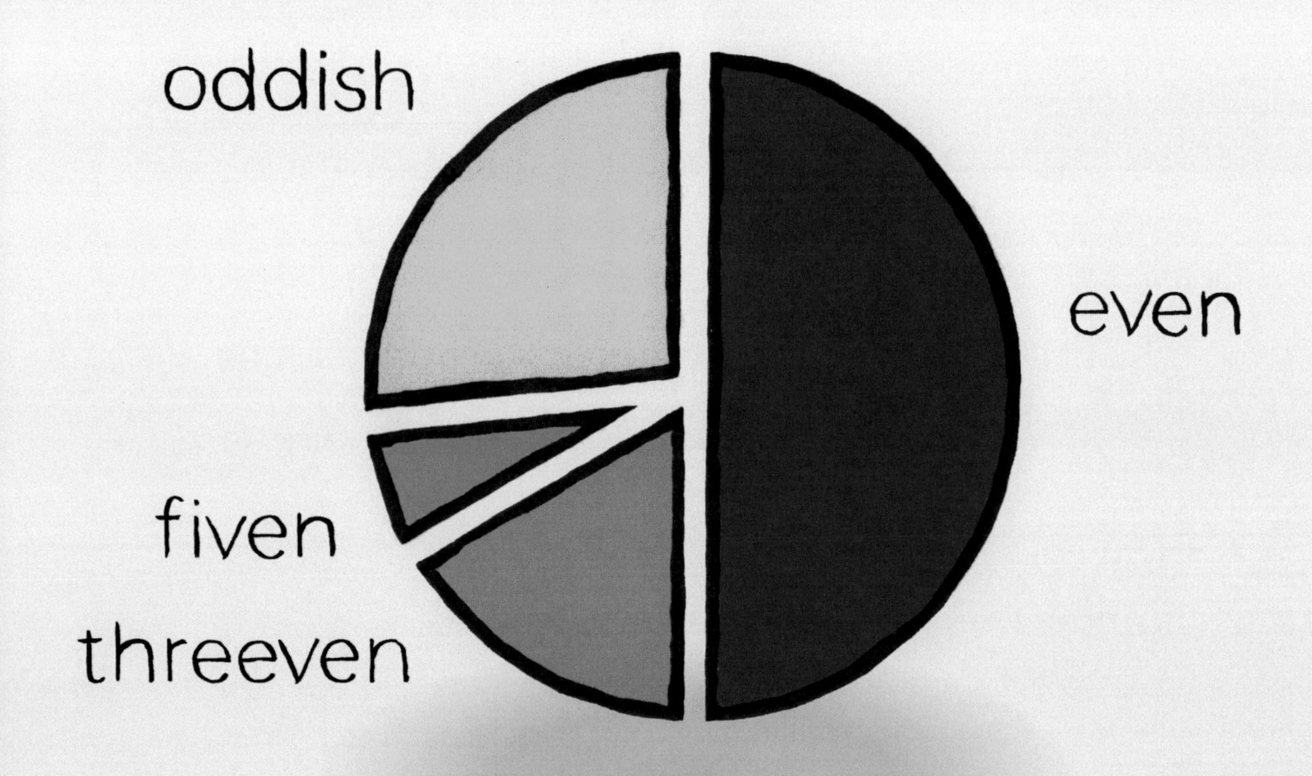

Fiven seemed a good name for this next list and the oddish list became smaller again.

Six, eight and ten all gave lists of only even numbers.

The list from counting in nines were all even or threeven.

However, seven made a new list and the oddish numbers reduced by another seventh.

7, 49, 77, 91, 119, 133 …

Eleven also made a new list using an eleventh of the remaining oddish numbers.

11, 121, 143, 187, 209 …

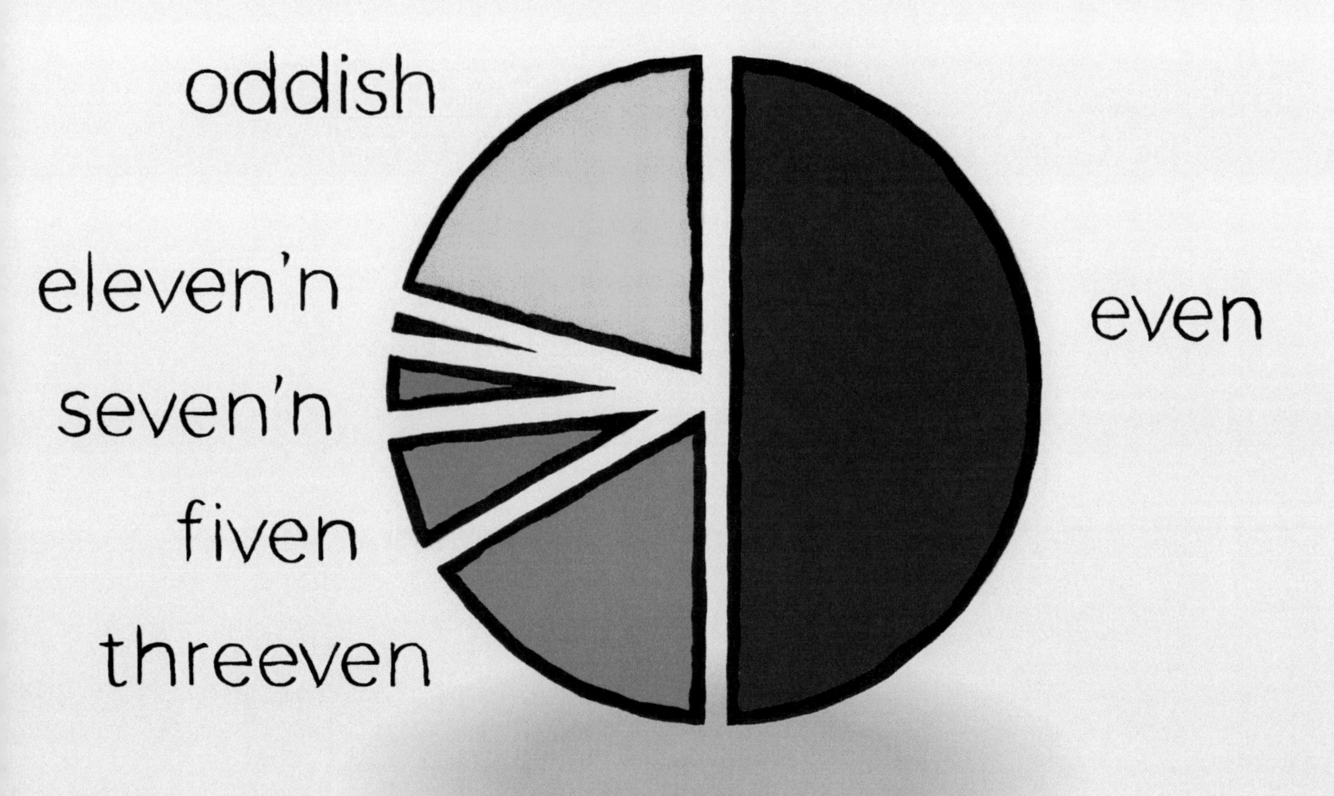

Emily had learnt about prime numbers at school. Looking proudly at her new lists, she saw each one started with a prime.

The word 'prime' is a borrowed French term and comes from the Latin *primus*, meaning first or distinguished. It has been used since the 16th century to describe a number that can only be divided by 1 and itself.

In the next list, thirteen'n, the numbers looked like they were going to get quite large.

And Emily imagined she could go on and on making new lists starting with primes.

$\frac{1}{2}$	$\frac{1}{6}$	$\frac{2}{30}$
even	threeven	fiven

It was proved in the 3rd century BC that the list of primes is infinite. The sequence shown by the numerators (top of the fractions) can also be made by the multiplication of each successive 'prime minus one'.

Every new list made up a smaller portion of all the numbers than the last.

Emily worked hard on her multiplications to show the size of each of her lists as a fraction.

$$\frac{8}{210}$$

seven'n

$$\frac{48}{2{,}310}$$

eleven'n

The denominators sequence (bottom of the fractions) can be re-created by multiplying successive primes. The numbers in this second sequence are known as 'primorials', a term coined in the 20th century.

even

1	2
3	4
5	6
7	8
9	10
11	12
13	14
15	16
17	18
19	20

Emily was keen to understand how these new lists fitted together when she counted all the numbers again, starting from one.

The odd and even numbers came together easily.

But including the threeven numbers was difficult without it looking like a jumble.

After trying a couple of different things, Emily found that rows of six made everything neat and tidy.

threeven

1	2	3	4	5	6
7	8	9	10	11	12
13	14	15	16	17	18
19	20	21	22	23	24
25	26	27	28	29	30
31	32	33	34	35	36
37	38	39	40	41	42
43	44	45	46	47	48
49	50	51	52	53	54
55	56	57	58	59	60

There was one threeven number in every six numbers - just like the fraction!

When Emily went to include the fiven numbers she looked at the fractions first and built her list with rows of thirty.

There were two fiven numbers in each row - always in the same position. And all the bigger primes were in the oddish columns.

Emily realised that her notepad wasn't wide enough to include the seven'n and eleven'n numbers in tidy columns, let alone the bigger primes.

The 'twin prime conjecture' proposes that there are an infinite number of pairs of primes separated by a gap of one. This threeven pattern shows how this might be so, with oddish numbers either side of every sixth number.

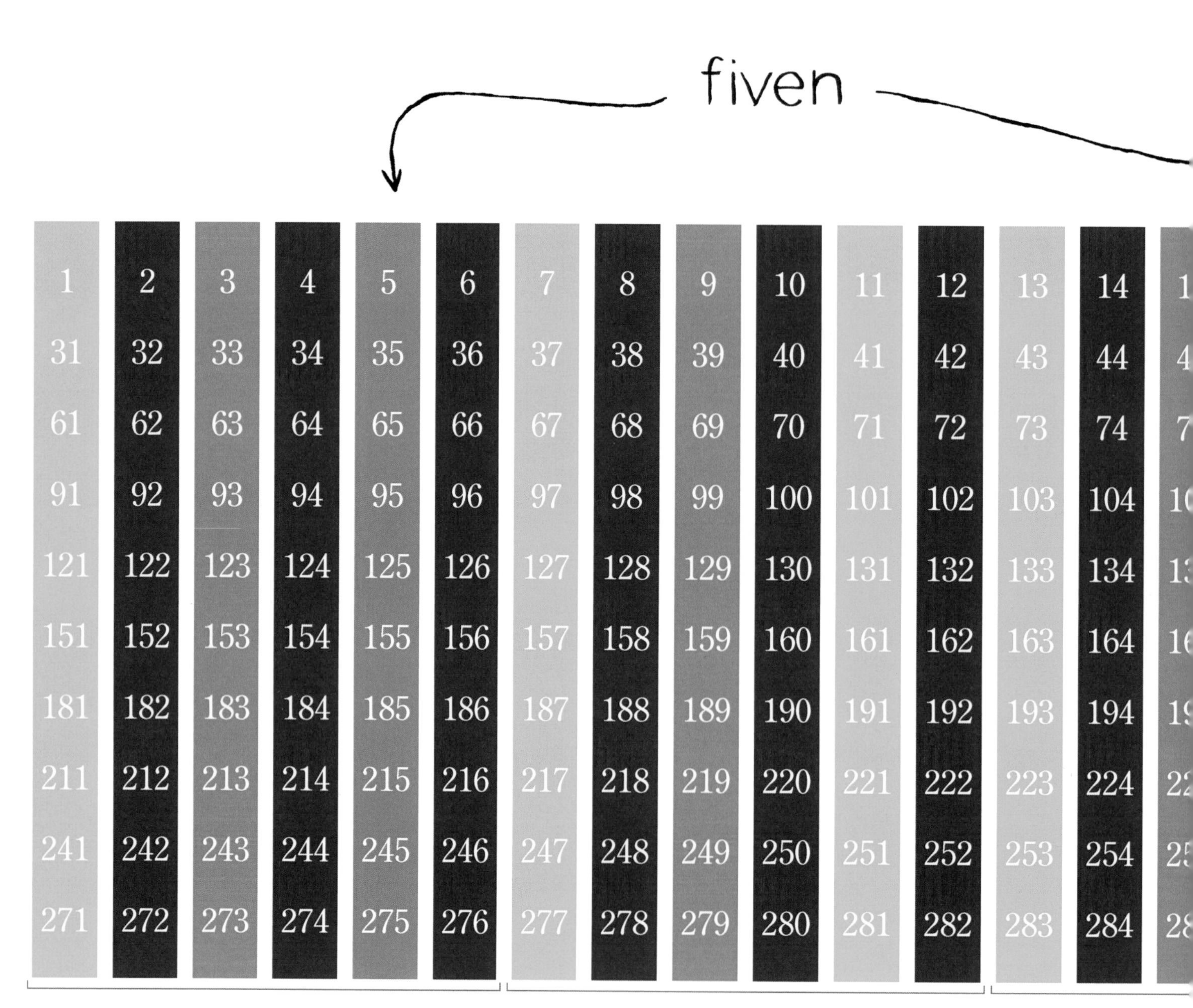

Each of these repeating sequences of oddish numbers (in gold) are, in fact, symmetrical if an additional zero column is imagined on the left-hand side.

6	17	18	19	20	21	22	23	24	25	26	27	28	29	30
6	47	48	49	50	51	52	53	54	55	56	57	58	59	60
6	77	78	79	80	81	82	83	84	85	86	87	88	89	90
06	107	108	109	110	111	112	113	114	115	116	117	118	119	120
36	137	138	139	140	141	142	143	144	145	146	147	148	149	150
66	167	168	169	170	171	172	173	174	175	176	177	178	179	180
96	197	198	199	200	201	202	203	204	205	206	207	208	209	210
26	227	228	229	230	231	232	233	234	235	236	237	238	239	240
56	257	258	259	260	261	262	263	264	265	266	267	268	269	270
86	287	288	289	290	291	292	293	294	295	296	297	298	299	300

The pattern symmetry ensures that the positions either side of the primorial, and multiples of the primorial, will always be candidates for primes - and another source of twin primes.

Emily could now see a pattern in all the lists except the oddish numbers, which were still a bit messy.

The list of oddish numbers got smaller when a prime list was removed. But it would never disappear completely as it always started with one.

Did this mean one was a prime number?

The oddish numbers greater than one were the bigger primes and their products - all mixed together.

Emily used her chalk board to write out each oddish list until she came to a number she knew wasn't prime.

all	odd	threeven oddish
1	1	1
2	3	5
3	5	7
4	7	11
	9	13
		17
		19
		23
		25

fiven oddish

1
7
11
13
17
19
23
29
31
37
41
43
47
49

seven'n oddish

1	
11	67
13	71
17	73
19	79
23	83
29	89
31	97
37	101
41	103
43	107
47	109
53	113
59	121
61	

eleven'n oddish

1		
13	71	139
17	73	149
19	79	151
23	83	157
29	89	163
31	97	167
37	101	169
41	103	
43	107	
47	109	
53	113	
59	127	
61	131	
67	137	

Every time she started a new list, a prime was removed from the top.

The numbers at the beginning of each oddish list were more likely to be primes. Further down they were more likely to be products of primes.

But for an unbroken section, at the start of each list, all the numbers were primes.

Emily now had everything she needed to create a list of the prime numbers.

In any oddish sequence, the first number after one will always be the next prime and the first non-prime will always be the square of that prime. The intervening numbers will all be prime.

Between one & four

Between four & nine

Between nine & twenty-five

Between twenty-five & forty-nine

Between forty-nine & one hundred and twenty-one

Between one hundred and twenty-one & one hundred and sixty-nine

The first 6 primes (2, 3, 5, 7, 11, 13) allow 33 more prime numbers to be calculated. Primes up to the 60th (281) can calculate 7683 ahead and primes to the 600th (4409) give more than a million further primes.

every number is prime,

2 & 3

the odd numbers are prime,

5 & 7

the odd numbers less the threeven list are prime,

11, 13, 17, 19 & 23

the remaining oddish numbers less the fiven list are prime,

29, 31, 37, 41, 43 & 47

the remaining oddish numbers less the seven'n list are prime,

53, 59, 61, 67, 71, 73, 79, 83, 89, 97, 101, 103, 107, 109 & 113

the remaining oddish numbers less the eleven'n list are prime.

127, 131, 137, 139, 149, 151, 157, 163 & 167

And so on. Forever.

So the primes are not perfectly round pebbles scattered on a never-ending beach.

Each new prime fills the first oddish gap left by the previous primes and their products.

The position of these gaps has already been decided. The primes just fall into them.

‘A prime number is not a product of itself or other numbers.’

Emily felt sad, at first, that one was not allowed to be in the club.

After all, everything had started with one.

But, then again, it is quite special to be one's own product.

All the integers are made from 1s. Each integer is 1 greater than its smaller neighbour and 1 smaller than its greater neighbour.

Joss Langford is often an engineer, sometimes a scientist and occasionally just plain difficult. He'd been noodling with prime numbers in the odd coffee break for eighteen months when he was diagnosed with throat cancer in 2017. This book has become part of his treatment and 30% of the publisher's proceeds will be donated to Somerset Unit for Radiotherapy Equipment.